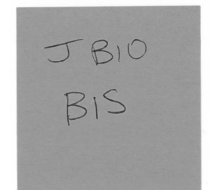

ISABELLA BIRD BISHOP

Anne Gatti

Hamish Hamilton
London

IN HER OWN TIME

This series focuses a spotlight on women whose lives and work have all too often been overlooked yet who have made significant contributions to society in many different areas: from politics and painting to science and social reform.

Women's voices have in the past been the silent ones of history. In Britain, for example, the restrictions of society, the time-consuming nature of domestic work, and the poor educational opportunities available to women until this century, have meant that not only did women rarely have the opportunity to explore their abilities beyond those which society expected of them, but also that their aspirations and achievements were often not recorded.

This series profiles a number of women who, through a combination of character and circumstance, were able to influence ideas and attitudes or contribute to the arts and sciences. None of them were alone in their ambitions. There must have been many other women whose experiences we know nothing of because they were not recorded. Many of the 'ordinary' women who have supported the so-called 'exceptional' women of history also displayed great courage, skill and determination. Political and social change, in particular, has been accelerated by the pioneering work of individual women but rarely achieved without the collective efforts of masses of unknown women.

The work of many women in the series took them into the public eye: some were honoured and celebrated, more frequently they faced disapproval or lack of sympathy with their ideas. Many were ahead of their time and only later did their pioneering activities gain public respect. Others found their lives so deeply entangled with current events that their path was virtually chosen for them. A few were not closely involved with contemporary society but highly original characters who nevertheless influenced or informed others. By exploring the struggles, hopes, failures and achievements of these women, we can discover much about the society they lived in and how each made their personal contribution — in their own way, in their own time.

Olivia Bennett

HAMISH HAMILTON CHILDREN'S BOOKS
Penguin Books Ltd, 27 Wrights Lane, London W8 5TZ (Publishing & Editorial)
and Harmondsworth, Middlesex, England (Distribution & Warehouse)
Viking Penguin Inc., 40 West 23rd Street, New York, New York 10010, U.S.A.
Penguin Books Australia Ltd, Ringwood, Victoria, Australia
Penguin Books Canada Limited, 2801 John Street, Markham, Ontario, Canada L3R 1B4
Penguin Books (N.Z.) Ltd, 182–190 Wairau Road, Auckland 10, New Zealand

First published in Great Britain 1988 by
Hamish Hamilton Children's Books

Copyright © 1988 by Anne Gatti

Design by Sally Boothroyd
Cover design by Clare Truscott
Maps by Tony Garrett

British Library Cataloguing in Publication Data:

Gatti, Anne
Isabella Bird Bishop.—(In her own time).
1. Bird, Isabella B.—Juvenile literature
2. Travellers—Great Britain—Biography
—Juvenile literature
I. Title   II. Series
910.4'092'4   G246.B5
ISBN 0-241-12150-7

Filmset in Palatino by
Katerprint Typesetting Services, Oxford
Printed in Great Britain by
Butler & Tanner, Frome, Somerset

Within quotations we have
retained Isabella Bird Bishop's
original spellings, which may
differ from those given
elsewhere in the text.

Contents

Chapter One

A Frail Child

The time is June 1873, the place is the side of the world's largest volcano, in Hawaii. Half way up is a middle-aged Victorian woman. All around her, on the jagged mountainside, are streams of burning lava. She scrambles up slopes which are so steep that her pack-horse stumbles and rolls backwards. Even her sure-footed mule falls twice. She jumps over deep cracks which look as if they drop straight down to the red-hot sea of lava. She finally reaches the top of the crater and looks down. She is mesmerised by what she calls the 'blackness and horror' of this vast hole.

Aged forty-one, Isabella Bird is on the first of many exciting and exhausting journeys to remote parts of the world, to places which few men, let alone women, have explored. Yet this is someone who only three years earlier was so frail that her doctor suggested she should wear a steel support at the back of her head to help her to sit up in bed. She was in pain for much of her life, yet travelling (and the rougher it was the better) was the one thing that could distract her. Her trips abroad — on horse, mule, yak or elephant — became the most important and enjoyable part of her life. After forty years of the quiet existence thought suitable for the unmarried daughter of a Victorian country parson, Isabella had discovered her true role — she was a born traveller.

Travelling unchaperoned to some of the remotest parts of the world, Isabella expressed her disregard for Victorian convention. This attitude was at times reflected in the clothes she wore. From time to time she would exchange her plain and sensible tweeds and flannels for lavishly embroidered silk outfits, such as this one from Manchuria in China, which she had brought back from her travels. She also had a special riding suit, which allowed her to ride astride a horse, not demurely sidesaddle as was customary for Victorian women.

Childhood

Isabella Bird was born on 15 October 1831 in a comfortable, middle-class home in Yorkshire. Her father was a pastor and her mother a Sunday school teacher. She and her younger sister Henrietta (whom she always called Hennie) were educated at home by their parents. As soon as the girls could read they sat down to lessons in literature, history, drawing, French, Latin, botany and the Scriptures. Isabella's parents realised that she was exceptionally bright when they found her, aged only seven, lying in the stables glued to an adult history book about the French Revolution.

The Bird household was a deeply religious one. Even on holiday their day began with the children and servants gathered for a reading from the Bible and morning prayers. On Sundays they spent several hours in church at morning and evening services. As for most Victorian children, saying prayers, going to church, doing good works and obeying your parents were all part of their Christian duty.

Isabella's parents, Edward and Dora Bird, were devout Christians who had strong moral convictions. Her father gave fiery sermons against the evils of Sunday trading and her aunts refused to take sugar in their tea as a protest against slave-grown products.

They were taught by visiting missionary friends of the family that there were other, 'less fortunate' people in the world who did not believe in the God of the Christian faith. It was the missionaries' job, they were told, to save these people's souls by turning them into good Christians.

Fighting pain

As a young girl Isabella developed a spinal disease but refused to give in to this handicap. With great courage, she forced herself to ride, run and climb with her sister and cousins. Because she was so frail she was told to spend as much time in the open air as possible. So, when her father did his parish rounds on horseback, he took her with him. Although she was still a small girl, she did not ride a pony as you might expect, but a fully-grown carriage horse. Like all females at the time, she rode sidesaddle.

Her father introduced her to all the wild plants, crops and animals in the area. He showed her how to measure the distance between places and objects just by using her eyes. It was on these rides that Isabella learnt the art of accurate observation, a skill that she later put to very good use with her travel writing, photography and drawings.

When Isabella was eleven her father was moved to a parish in Birmingham. She enthusiastically taught a class of Sunday school children but was not happy in the cramped, dirty city. She was at her best when she was on holiday with her family, tramping the remote highlands of Scotland. Even at this young age her health and mood seemed to be strongly affected by the environment around her.

When Isabella was eighteen she had an operation on her spine. Although her back was less painful afterwards, her health was still bad. She complained of vague aches and pains, insomnia and of feeling low. There's no doubt that she must have had a great deal of back pain at various times in her life but much of her poor health at this stage was probably caused by her mental state. She was in low spirits because she was frustrated: she was highly intelligent but as a woman could not use her mind in a way that stretched it. There was no university for her to go to (the first women's college was not opened until some twenty years later), and no acceptable profession for her to join. Middle-class

Had her courage not ridden above it, she might have delivered herself over to confirmed ill-health and adorned a sofa all her days. But even as a child, her brave spirit scorned prolonged concession to this delicacy.

Anna Stoddart, The Life of Isabella Bird, *1906*

Boroughbridge Hall in North Yorkshire where Isabella spent her early childhood.

women were expected to be homemakers, devoted wives and mothers.

Isabella wanted a challenge but where would she find it, as she sat in a parsonage drawing-room, entertaining callers, doing a little needlework or reading poetry? She knew that by the standards of the society she belonged to she *ought* to be happy. After all, she had loving parents, a comfortable home, no worries about feeding or clothing herself. But she wasn't, and so she felt guilty.

Fortunately, Isabella's doctor realised that her problems were as much psychological as physical. So, he prescribed a sea voyage. This was a common remedy offered to single women who were convalescing or seemed to be 'out of sorts'. At the age of eighteen, this small, delicate young Englishwoman, who had never travelled further than Scotland, packed her bags for America and Canada. Her father gave her £100 and told her not to come back until she had spent it all.

Chapter Two

First Travels

On the seat in front of me were two 'prairie-men'; tall, handsome . . . with brown curling hair and beards. They wore leather jackets, slashed and embroidered, leather smallclothes, large boots with embroidered tops, silver spurs, and caps of scarlet cloth . . . Dullness fled from their presence; they could tell stories, whistle melodies, and sing comic songs without cessation: fortunate were those near enough to be enlivened by their drolleries . . .

Isabella Bird Bishop

Almost as soon as Isabella landed in Nova Scotia, on the east coast of Canada, her aches and pains seemed to disappear. She travelled as far west as Chicago, as far south as Kentucky and returned north via New York. She threw herself into the trip wholeheartedly.

In Nova Scotia she rattled along in a battered coach over roads made out of pine trunks and swapped ghost stories with the coachman. In Boston she was dazzled by the luxury of her hotel parlour where 'a fountain of antique workmanship threw up a jet d'eau of iced water scented with eau-de-Cologne'. In Chicago her accommodation was a flea-ridden inn where she sat down to a shared meal of 'eight boiled legs of mutton, nearly raw; six antiquated fowls, whose legs were of the consistency of guitar strings; baked pork with "onion fixings", the meat swimming in grease'. The diners hacked at the joints and then dipped their greasy knives straight into the salt pot as there were no such things as salt spoons.

Although Isabella was not used to such unhygienic conditions she stuck it out. She quickly realised that she would get much more out of her travels if she grabbed whatever new experience came her way, good or bad. 'Though I certainly felt rather out of my element in this place,' she wrote, 'I was not at all sorry for the opportunity . . . of seeing something of America in its lowest grade.'

The opening page of Isabella's first book, The Englishwoman in America, *which was published anonymously in 1856. There was a gap of nineteen years before her next book,* Six Months in the Sandwich Islands, *came out.*

All along the trip Isabella had been writing notes and sending long, descriptive letters to her family and friends. When she returned to her parents' home in Huntingdonshire, she used these to write her first travel book which she called *The Englishwoman in America*. Writing was an acceptable pastime for a Victorian woman and Isabella had no difficulty in finding a publisher. Her trip to America had given her the chance to travel unchaperoned, which she could not possibly have done in England — American ladies had much more freedom in this respect. It also allowed her to make use of her talent for sharp observation and vivid descriptive writing.

Life in Scotland

When Isabella was twenty-nine her father died and the family moved to Edinburgh. Here she became involved in various charitable works. Most of her energy went into helping the Scottish crofters in the Hebrides. They were living in damp, overcrowded cottages which they had to share with their livestock. Ever since the blight of their potato crops in the 1840s they had been desperately short of food. Isabella used money from the publication of her book to buy them fishing boats and equipment to make tweed cloth. She helped many other crofters to emigrate to Canada and America.

A shipowner, who watched Isabella helping a number of emigrating families to embark, was impressed with the way she organised them, not officiously but sympathetically: 'The sadness at leaving their native shores had given place to cheerfulness — due to Miss Bird's presence among them . . . There was something about Miss Bird that filled every one with whom she came in contact with a desire to serve her.' Later in her life, Isabella was to inspire many people — guides, interpreters, coolies — with the same devotion.

Gradually Isabella found herself slipping back into the life of a semi-invalid, spending mornings in bed writing articles for worthy magazines or studying poetry. When her mother died in 1866 Isabella turned to Hennie, her sister, for comfort and friendship. The two sisters shared a holiday cottage on the Hebridean island of Mull. Hennie was shy and gentle with none of Isabella's drive or ambition. She led a quiet life, painting, studying Greek and Latin, and, like Isabella, did 'good works'.

Isabella greatly admired selfless people like Hennie who seemed content to devote themselves to good causes for the rest of their lives. Her upbringing told her that this was the right thing to do but her personality made it increasingly difficult for her to put into practice. To add to her troubles, she continued to be ill and suffered 'choking, aching, leeches, poultices, doctors twice a day'. She grew more and more depressed.

Again, her doctor recommended a sea journey. Isabella chose a cruise which would take her to New York and back via the Mediterranean. But she was too ill to leave the boat and returned feeling worse. Still the only remedy the doctors could suggest was travel. So, in the summer of 1872, when Isabella was forty and desperate for a cure, she set off on a round-the-world trip.

A challenge at last

By the time she reached Australia Isabella was in a terrible state. Australia, she told

Isabella's sister Hennie was gentle, shy and a model of charity and kindness. She was content to lead a quiet, devout life in Edinburgh and on the island of Mull whereas Isabella was easily frustrated by such an uneventful life.

Hennie in her letters, was hot, dusty and full of hysterical ladies and gossiping clergymen. New Zealand was not much better. In Auckland she boarded a dilapidated old paddle steamer bound for California and from then on things began to improve. On the second day the boat was nearly wrecked by a hurricane; a young man became seriously ill and Isabella helped to nurse him; and there was the daily threat of engine failure. All these dangers, and the excitement of not knowing what each day would bring, cheered Isabella up most effectively.

Here was the kind of challenge that Isabella had been hoping for. The social restrictions of middle-class Edinburgh seemed far away. She wrote home, 'It is so like living in a new world, so free . . . so unfettered . . . there can be nothing to annoy one — no door-bells, no "please mems", no bills, no demands of any kind.'

Isabella had found a new lease of life. When the mother of the sick passenger asked if she would disembark with her at the Sandwich Islands (now the American state of Hawaii) Isabella thought 'why not?', and accepted.

Manual labour, a rough life and freedom from conventionalities added to novelty would be a good thing.

Isabella Bird Bishop (on the kind of life she would enjoy)

Sailing in the Sandwich Islands

14

Chapter Three

At the Top of a Volcano

As the paddle steamer chugged into
Honolulu harbour on the island of Oahu,
Isabella and the other passengers were given
an exotic welcome. Canoes raced out to meet
them, naked islanders splashed about in the
sea, waving. Standing on the quay other
islanders, swathed in garlands of tropical
flowers, called out in their unfamiliar
language.

Isabella was delighted to see that a group
of foreign ladies were wearing simple muslin
dresses. She had little time for what she
called 'the humpings and bunchings . . . and

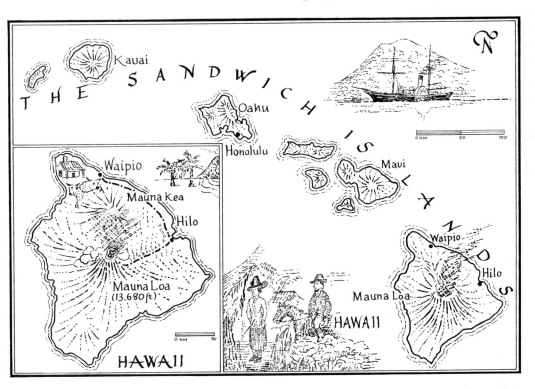

deformities of ultra fashionable bad taste'. By that she meant the tightly-laced whalebone corsets, layers of thick petticoats, heavily-padded sleeves and bodices that were all the fashion in England at the time. These 'deformities', especially crinolines (steel cages worn by society ladies under their dresses to make them billow out), made it difficult for women to sit or walk comfortably.

Isabella quickly grew tired of the respectable life in the island's only hotel and headed for Hilo on the lesser-known island of Hawaii. Hilo lay on a bay of silken sand, fringed with palm trees and heady flowers. It had about thirty foreign settlers, three churches, a court house and a few general stores. She stayed at the home of the American sheriff and was greatly taken with the free-and-easy way of life there which allowed plenty of time for reading, music, fern printing and riding.

Isabella loved horses but riding sidesaddle on rough ground painfully jarred her spine.

An illustration from Punch *1858 showing a lady in a billowing crinoline. Apart from being very awkward to wear, crinolines were dangerous: some women were burnt to death when their crinolines caught fire. Isabella hated the restrictions on women's comfort and movement which Victorian high fashion demanded.*

At Hilo she was offered a sturdy Mexican saddle, ideal for dealing with Hawaii's rocky paths. However, to ride astride Isabella would need a special riding outfit. So her friends made one for her. It consisted of baggy bloomers gathered in at the ankles and covered by a long skirt which fell either side of the saddle, hiding the bloomers completely.

Isabella was liberated. At last she could gallop in comfort. But she took care to switch to sidesaddle whenever she came to a town, in case she might offend people who had never seen a woman riding astride. She felt, as did most Victorian women of her class, that a woman must always be ladylike. It's no wonder, then, that she was furious when *The Times* later accused her of having worn 'masculine habiliments'. She wrote indignantly to her publisher saying that the riding dress was commonly worn by 'English and American *ladies* in Hawaii' (in other words, by 'respectable' women).

Exploring the islands

Booted and spurred, shaded by a broad-rimmed Australian hat, Isabella started to explore. She headed north along the coast, with two young native guides, towards the beautiful Waipio valley. The route was a dangerous one, over rocky peaks which dropped down to deep ravines. The only way across was by sliding down almost vertical winding paths and wading the fast-flowing streams.

Isabella was, quite literally, thrown in at the deep end and on one occasion was lucky to make it. She and her guides plunged into a torrent and found the force of the river almost too strong for their horses: 'With

As I find that a lady can travel alone with perfect safety, I have many projects in view, but whatever I do or plan to do, I find my eyes always turning to the light on the top of Mauna Loa. I know that the ascent is not feasible for me . . . but that glory, nearly 14,000 feet [4267 m] aloft, . . . has an intolerable fascination.

Isabella Bird Bishop,
Six Months in the Sandwich Islands

A FOREST STREAM IN KAUAI.

wilder fury the river rushed by, its waters whirled dizzily and, in spite of spurring and lifting with the rein, the horses were swept seawards . . . only the horses' heads and our own heads and shoulders were above the water . . .'

Eventually, Isabella and her mare reached the far side. She found that she was trembling all over. She had, she realised, narrowly escaped death. Later she wrote to Hennie that having survived this experience she now felt able to 'ride anywhere and any distance'.

Up in the high tableland behind Waipio Isabella met cattle-raising settlers. There were ex-whalers, sheep-shearers, cabin boys, farmhands, office boys and trappers who had come from places as far apart as London, Tasmania, the Canadian Rockies and the Mississippi. Many of them had landed on Hawaii by chance, had liked what they saw and stayed.

Here Isabella was introduced to a Mr Wilson, jack-of-all-trades. He was rather taken with this fearless, intelligent woman who could discuss the price of wool or the raising of bullocks as knowledgeably as any man. But when, after a few meetings, he proposed to her, Isabella shied away. Although she thought he was 'a splendid looking fellow', she would not consider the idea of a serious involvement and sped back to Honolulu.

She was drawn like a magnet to Hawaii's towering volcano, Mauna Loa, but that could wait for the moment. Determined to see more of the islands she boarded a schooner for Kauai. Kauai was a paradise to her, small and fertile with only a handful of foreigners. She was strongly tempted to stay. But after three blissful months she got her usual itchy feet and decided to move on, this time back to Hilo and the challenge of Mauna Loa.

A remarkable climb

Very few men and, Isabella was told, only one woman, had reached the top of the world's largest volcano. An Englishman called Mr Green was planning to climb it and Isabella asked to accompany him. Although it would have been highly unacceptable in England for an unmarried woman to travel, unchaperoned, with an unknown gentleman, here on Hawaii no one gave it a second thought. Partly because she was so respectable and partly because she was now recognised as a serious traveller, Isabella was

Part of a letter from Isabella to Hennie written from Mauna Loa on Hawaii and dated 6 June 1873. She is describing another of the island's volcanoes, Mauna Kea, which has been active for three months. 'Mr Green [her companion] measured the number of seconds which the lava took to fall from the highest elevation to which it was thrown, and it varied from 150 to 300 feet but there was one outburst soon after midnight when it was fully 500 feet!'

free to go wherever she wanted — alone or with whoever she chose. She loved this freedom. The more travelling she did, the more independent and solitary she became — the only person she seemed strongly attached to was Hennie.

Equipped with woollen stockings, a Mexican poncho, a camping blanket and kettle, she set off with Mr Green. They climbed, on mules, into the frozen, craggy mountains. After hours of slipping and scrambling they reached the edge of the crater. They gazed in silence at this black hole which was over nine kilometres round. It was throwing up fountains of fire. Jets of gold and red criss-crossed the sky like the most glorious fireworks display imaginable. Although Isabella was dizzy with vertigo and her hands were almost paralysed with the cold, she took out her pen and paper and started to describe to Hennie what she saw.

To Hennie, and to the people who later bought the book she wrote, Isabella's role was more than that of a writer. As her readers had no television, no radio, no colour photos (black-and-white photography was still experimental), Isabella's words had to paint a technicolour picture of the volcano for them. She had to make them feel the scorching heat of the lava, smell the stench of sulphur, hear the thunderous roar of lava explosions and see, in all its details, one of nature's most exciting spectacles. In fact, her role was that of a television documentary maker of today.

She managed to do this very successfully and her book *Six Months in the Sandwich Islands* was an instant hit. The magazine *The Spectator* described it as 'remarkable, fascinating and beautifully written'.

Chapter Four

Romance in the Rockies

. . . in the course of my somewhat extensive travels in the United States, and mixing as I did very frequently with the lower classes, I never heard any of that language which so frequently offends the ear in England. I must not be misunderstood here. Profane language is only too notoriously common in the States, but custom . . . totally prohibits its use before ladies.

Isabella Bird Bishop

Isabella's next port of call was San Francisco. In the dusty summer heat she disembarked and boarded the first available train heading east. She had heard about a remote and beautiful valley at the foot of the Rocky Mountains in Colorado called Estes Park.

She left the train at the prairie town of Greeley and got a place in a cart bound for the Rockies. Twenty years before Isabella arrived, Colorado had belonged to Indians. Then a handful of fur trappers had trekked into the Rockies in search of beaver, and stayed. Some of them set up home with Indian women and remained hunters, others settled down to farm the land and raise their families. Attacks by Indians were now rare, but life was still tough for these pioneers.

In a letter to Hennie from the Rockies Isabella describes the excitement of her first encounter with a mountain eagle: 'A huge thing . . . with beating wings came sailing towards me . . . it passed only about three feet over my head. I saw for the first time the gigantic mountain eagle carrying a good-sized beast in his talons!'

Isabella found the prairie towns rough and dirty. They were filled, she said, with drunk and brawling settlers. At Longmount she met two young men who were going to Estes. Together they crossed the prairie, rode through canyons and streams and up into the valley of Estes Park. It was not a tame park in the English sense but a wild grassy valley, twenty-nine kilometres long, enclosed not by walls but by forest-covered mountains. The park was home to beavers, deer, skunks, grizzly bears, coyotes, lynx and a few trappers and cattle breeders.

Rocky Mountain Jim

At the entrance to the valley a collie stood beside the track, barking at the travellers. Its owner came out of a black log cabin which leaked smoke through its window and roof. He wore a tattered hunting suit, had a knife in his belt and a revolver in his breast pocket. With only one good eye (he had lost the other in a fight with a bear) and hair that curled down over his collar, he looked every bit the *desperado* he was famed to be. His name was Jim Nugent. Isabella was instantly impressed with his striking looks and unexpected charm. 'We entered into conversation, and as he spoke I forgot both his reputation and appearance, for his manner was that of a chivalrous gentleman, his accent refined, and his language easy and elegant.'

Before long Jim, who had run away as a youngster from his middle-class Canadian home and become a fur trapper and U.S. Army scout, came to call on Isabella. She was renting a log cabin nearby from a Welshman called Griff Evans. Jim offered to take her up Long's Peak, a 4200-metre mountain which dominated the skyline.

As we crept from the ledge round a horn of rock I beheld what made me perfectly sick and dizzy to look at — the terminal peak itself — a smooth, cracked face or wall of pink granite, as nearly perpendicular as anything could well be up which it was possible to climb . . . It took one hour to accomplish 500 feet [152 m], pausing for breath every minute or two.

Isabella Bird Bishop (on climbing Long's Peak)

They were joined by the two men who had arrived with Isabella. They climbed up through the dense pine forests and made camp at 3350 metres. As the temperature dropped below zero Isabella bedded down on thick pine shoots, using her upturned saddle for a pillow. Listening to the gusting wind and howling wolves, she was too excited to sleep.

The next morning the serious climbing started. When their route was blocked with ice and they had to climb down some 600 metres, slipping and bruising themselves all the way, Isabella told the others to go on without her. But Jim wouldn't hear of it and threatened to carry her to the top, if necessary. As it was, he half pulled her up, making steps for her with his hands and feet.

The last stretch was terrifyingly steep and

Griff Evans's ranch in Estes Park, Colorado. Isabella stayed in a small cabin of her own close to the main one which had 'a roughstone fireplace, in which pine logs, half as large as I am, were burning; a boarded floor, a round table, two rocking chairs . . . Skins, Indian bows and arrows . . . and antlers, fitly decorated the rough walls, and equally fitly, rifles were stuck in the corners.'

they had to stop every minute or so to catch their breath. The thin air at this height made breathing extremely painful. Their mouths were so dry that it was almost impossible to speak.

They reached the top and as Isabella looked down on the snow-capped Rockies, on rivers, lakes and miles of pine trees, she was 'uplifted above love and hate and storms of passion'. Nature's great sights always had a calming, almost spiritual effect on her.

Life on the ranch

Back at Griff's ranch, Isabella was happy and well, driving cattle with the men, sharing meals in the main cabin and listening to stories about Indians. She was also getting to known Jim Nugent better. Although she was aware of his reputation for drinking too much whisky, for picking violent fights and for being dangerously moody, she was fascinated by his store of wonderful tales, and by the poetry he wrote. She found him intelligent and witty and they often rode and talked together.

Isabella could sense a strong tension between Jim and Griff Evans. She felt that Griff was envious of Jim's reputation as the wild, romantic mountain man. Realising that her presence added to this tension, she decided to move on again. She set off by pony for Denver, the capital of Colorado. She stayed there just long enough to get letters of introduction from the ex-governor, before moving on again. These letters would make it possible for her to stay at the homes of various settlers along her route, for inns only existed in the towns.

She travelled south, on her own, as far as Colorado Springs and then west towards the

Rockies. She followed tracks of elk and shared a meal of venison with Commanche Bill, another *desperado* who spent most of his time killing Indians in revenge for his family who had been massacred by Cheyennes. One night she had to share a shed with drunken miners — for the first time she took out her revolver and slept with it against her cheek.

Returning to Denver, she found that the banks would not cash her travellers' notes. So she decided to go back to Estes Park to ask Griff for money that she had lent him. It was now nearly winter and she found only two cow-hands at the ranch. She mucked in, baking bread and helping with the cattle and horses. Jim Nugent reappeared and admitted

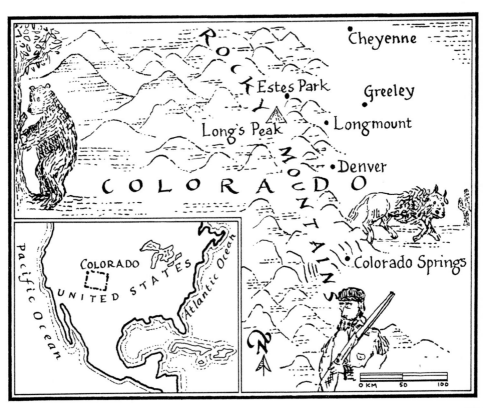

that as soon as she had gone he had realised he was 'attached' to her. They spent a lot of time together but their relationship was stormy. Jim was full of self pity about his wasted opportunities. Although he was clearly much taken with Isabella's plucky, intelligent and kind nature, it was too late, he said, to change his ways. Isabella felt sorry for him but told Hennie, 'I would not dare to trust my happiness to him because of the whisky.'

When Griff returned Isabella made a quick decision to leave. Jim gave her his finest beaver skin and accompanied her, in silence, to an inn where she boarded a waggon for Cheyenne. Six months later, Jim was dead, killed in a fight with Griff Evans.

Several years afterwards Isabella wrote to a friend, 'Don't let anybody think that I was in love with Mountain Jim.' Certainly in her book about the trip there's no mention of their feelings for each other. But Isabella's letters to Hennie tell a different story. They reveal her nervousness about Jim's strong feelings for her and about her feelings for him. When he confessed that 'he was attached to me and it was killing him . . . I was terrified . . . He is a man whom any woman might love but whom no sane woman would marry.'

Back in Edinburgh, Isabella took an advanced course in botany. She also helped to organise a shelter for the city's cab drivers and spent quiet summers in Hennie's cottage on the Isle of Mull. But once again, she began to have headaches, fevers and more back pain. The doctors advised travel and this time she set herself a specific task: to make a careful record of one of the world's more remote countries. She chose Japan.

After baking the bread and thoroughly cleaning the churns and pails, I began upon the tins and pans . . and was hard at work, very greasy and grimy, when a man came to know where to ford the river . . . he looked pityingly at me, saying 'Be you the new hired girl? Bless me, you're awful small!'

Isabella Bird Bishop (on being mistaken for a cleaning girl)

I always feel dil (dull and inactive) when I am stationary. . . . When I am travelling I don't feel it, but that is why I can never stay anywhere.

Isabella Bird Bishop

26

Chapter Five

The Real Japan

By spring 1878, when Isabella disembarked at the bustling port of Yokohama, Japan had been open to Western trading ships and visitors for just over twenty-five years. For over two hundred years before that, not a single Western ship had been allowed to drop anchor along its coastline.

It was amazing how quickly Western influence had spread once the ports were opened. Isabella noticed railway stations, banks, post offices, factories, even people wearing morning suits and top hats. But this was not what she had come to see. After one day in the city she longed to get away into the 'real Japan'. By that she meant the forests and villages of the interior which most Westerners did not bother to visit.

Dressed in her 'travelling costume' of striped tweed, a bamboo hat and laced boots, she headed north to the magnificent holy shrines at Nikko. Ito, a youth of eighteen, was her guide and interpreter. At Nikko she experienced oriental village life for the first time. Her room was simply yet beautifully furnished, right down to a single spray of flowers carefully arranged in a white vase. Its perfection made her nervous about spilling a drop of ink! Everyday life outside her room seemed equally peaceful and ordered.

After Nikko, though, the road became a rough, twisty trail through rocks and marshes. The villages consisted of clusters of shabby huts with manure heaps piled up in front of them. Isabella was quite shocked at

Mrs Bishop has never been deterred from any undertaking by its discomforts or dangers, and yet we do not remember ever having heard that she laid claim to or received any consideration on account of her sex.

The Spectator

the sight of the villagers who were half
naked, their skin crusted with sores and dirt.
She herself was soon covered in insect bites.
Her diet of mouldy rice, soggy sago and eggs
didn't give her much nourishment. By the
time she reached the northern town of
Kubota she was greatly relieved to be offered
a beef steak dinner.

Kubota was a hive of traditional activities
such as bamboo weaving and silk
manufacturing. But even here Western
influence had crept in. There was a new

28

hospital which used Western medicines and a school where chemistry, physics and Western economic theory replaced the teaching of Japanese literature and martial arts. Isabella was given a warm welcome but was most put out to discover that the pupils were not being introduced to Christianity. To her, there was no point in teaching them Western scientific or economic ideas unless they were also told, as she had been, of God's infinite wisdom and love, and of the importance of being a good Christian.

As a child, Isabella had been taught that all heathens (non-Christians) were lost souls, never able to enter Heaven. As she travelled on, and met more and more non-Christians, she began to wonder whether God might, after all, let the good heathen in. She made an effort to understand Buddhism, Japan's national religion, by spending some time with a Buddhist priest. But for her the Buddhist ideas of rebirth and enlightenment were confusing and, in the end, 'empty of meaning and purpose'. She came away from Japan believing, as she had been brought up to believe, that the Christian religion was the only true faith.

I had not been long in bed on Saturday night when I was woken by Ito bringing in an old hen which he said he could stew till it was tender, and I fell asleep with its dying squeak in my ears, to be awoke a second time by two policemen wanting for some occult reason to see my passport, and a third time by two men with lanterns scrambling and fumbling about the room, for the strings of a mosquito net which they wanted for another traveller.

Isabella Bird Bishop (on a typical night's sleep in rural Japan)

Living with the Ainu

From the coast near Kubota Isabella took a boat across to the island of Hokkaido. She found a land that had only been half explored. It was peopled by a race called the Ainu, the original inhabitants of the Japanese islands. Japanese people from the cities, such as her guide Ito, considered them sub-human, not much better than dogs.

The Ainu had strong muscly bodies and thick black hair and beards. They made their clothes from tree bark and animal skins. They were illiterate and worshipped the bear, the sun, moon, fire and water. Most Victorians would have written them off as hopeless 'savages'. (By 'savage' they did not mean someone who was vicious or violent but an uneducated person, who knew nothing of the Christian God.) Isabella, on the other hand, was prepared to take a closer look at the Ainus' lives before judging them. In fact, she was immediately attracted to them. She had already broken one convention of her time by travelling alone into remote Japan. Now she was breaking a second by not dismissing the Ainu just because they were heathens.

Much to the annoyance of Ito, she insisted on staying in several Ainu settlements. At the largest village, she was given place of honour in the chief's thatched hut — she was, after all, the first foreign woman they had ever seen. She was surprised and delighted to find the village so neat and clean. She questioned them for many hours about their beliefs and customs. And, after the evening meal (a mush of wild roots, beans, seaweed and dried fish which she was not quite brave enough to try), she crept under her mosquito net to sleep, next to the chief and his family. For a moment, she admits, she felt a slight panic, 'as if I were incurring a risk by being alone among savages'. But she trusted her instincts and slept safely.

Isabella was touched by the Ainus' hospitality, by the way they respected their old people and by the way children instantly obeyed their parents. 'Surely,' she wrote to a friend, 'these simple savages are children, as children to be judged.' She was not upset that they were not Christians: in fact, she found the Ainu way of life 'considerably higher and better than that of thousands of

I am specially pleased that the reviewers have not made any puerile remarks on the feminine authorship of the book or awarded praise or blame on that score.

Isabella Bird Bishop (on Unbeaten Tracks in Japan)

the lapsed masses of our own great cities who are baptised in Christ's name . . . in as much as the Ainos are truthful and, on the whole, chaste, hospitable, honest, reverent and kind to the aged.' Later in her travels, however, Isabella became more typically Victorian and grew much less tolerant of what she called 'heathen savages'.

At the end of 1878, on the way home, Isabella stopped off at Canton in China. Here she visited the city's prison and execution site. Her detached, detailed descriptions of the prisoners, their bodies 'covered with vermin and running sores', and of the scraps of human remains at the execution site, show how tough, both mentally and physically, she must have been.

At Singapore a British official suggested she might like to take a look at the Malay States. Typically, Isabella jumped at the chance of exploring new territory.

The Malay States
The six weeks Isabella spent in the Malay States gave her first-hand experience of British government officials abroad. She visited several British Residents, who were supposed to advise local native rulers and help them to administer the law. Some, Isabella discovered, used their influence well; others seriously abused their position.

At Klang, the capital of the state of Selangor, she met a Resident who spent his time bullying the native Sultan and shooting wild birds. Further north, in the state of Perak, she set out for the Residency of Mr Hugh Low at Kuala Kangsa in the interior. Her journey there, through dense rain forest, was one of the slowest and most ludicrous she ever undertook.

The inside of an Ainu hut, similar to the one Isabella stayed in. The huts were made of straw and wood and the floors covered with reed mats. On her first visit Isabella was offered the place of honour on a platform which was raised one foot off the ground. However, when it was time to eat, she got out her portable chair and sat on it on the platform, 'to avoid the fleas, which are truly legion'.

Because of the danger of tigers, Isabella had been given an elephant to ride. She soon discovered that, without a moment's warning, the animal would suddenly stop, bend its knees and crash down. Isabella would have to dismount, the load would have to be rearranged and the elephant coaxed back into action.

After some hours the driver jumped off for a smoke. The elephant wandered into the jungle where, after tearing at trees, he found a mud hole. He 'drew all the water out of it, squirted it with a loud noise over himself and

32

his riders, soaking my clothes, and when he turned back to the road again he stopped . . . and when I hit him with my umbrella he uttered the loudest roar I ever heard.' Eventually, Isabella abandoned the struggle and walked the last twelve kilometres to Mr Low's bungalow.

Mr Low was away so Isabella dined, on the first night, in the company of his two pet apes. They ate, like her, from porcelain plates. However, the big one didn't always wait to be served — from time to time he'd just grab something from a dish as the butler passed by! Since Isabella loathed making small talk, she judged it a perfect meal.

When Mr Low returned Isabella was most impressed with his respectful manner towards the Malays. His doors were always open to the reigning prince, to the chiefs (who might ask for his help with a marauding tiger) or to Chinese miners (who were worried about outbreaks of the crippling disease *beri-beri*). Above all, she admired him for his lack of arrogance.

Reluctantly, Isabella decided it was time to return home.

Isabella had to ride an elephant through the Malayan jungle: 'This mode of riding is not comfortable. One sits facing forward with the feet dangling over the edge of the basket. This edge soon produces a sharp ache or cramp, and when one tries to get relief by leaning back on anything, the awkward, rolling motion is so painful, that one reverts to the former position till it again becomes intolerable.'

Chapter Six

Death and Marriage

The original cover of Unbeaten Tracks in Japan, *published in 1880.*

On her way back from the Far East, Isabella stopped off at Cairo where she caught a fever. She arrived in Scotland in May 1879, very weak and ill. However, she was delighted to see Hennie again and they spent a quiet, happy summer together on Mull. Isabella told a friend, at about this time, that she now knew she would always have to fight depression. She resolved to do this 'by earnest work, and by trying to lose myself in the interests of others'.

She spent the winter working hard on her book on Japan. Her publisher wanted her to 'tone down' her descriptions of Japanese peasant life. But she would not gloss over the more shocking descriptions: she had to 'speak the truth', she said. Meanwhile, her book about the Rocky Mountains had come out and was being praised to the skies.

The following summer Hennie caught typhoid and died. Isabella was shattered. 'She was *my world*', she wrote to a friend, 'the light . . . and inspiration of my life have died with her.' Hennie had always been waiting to welcome her when she returned from her trips. She was the one person with whom Isabella shared her true feelings.

Isabella was so wrapped up in her grief that she hardly noticed the compliments that were being showered on her latest book, *Unbeaten Tracks in Japan*. The book established her as a serious observer of society in the Far East. She was pleased, however, that the trip had proved to the world that a woman had the right 'to do what she can do well'. On all her journeys she was careful not to let any of her male companions regret that they had a woman in tow. In fact, she more than matched them in courage, endurance and determination.

A devoted husband

While Hennie was dying she had been nursed by John Bishop, a doctor friend of both sisters. He was a highly respected physician in Edinburgh who shared with Isabella a love for the microscopic study of plants. Some years earlier he had proposed to her but she had refused, saying that she was 'scarcely a marrying woman'.

John was kind-hearted, unselfish and devoted to Isabella. He kept by her side while she mourned Hennie's death and eventually Isabella agreed to marry him. However, she put one condition on the marriage: that she must be free 'for further outlandish travel' if she felt the need.

On 8 March 1881, when Isabella was fifty and John forty, they married. Isabella, however, didn't make much of an effort to make it a happy day: there were no wedding guests and she wore black. For the first few years of their marriage she was gloomy company. She seemed to think of little else except her 'abiding grief' for Hennie. She found the 'everyday drudgery' of keeping house in Edinburgh a further misery.

She was shaken out of her self-pity, however, when John fell ill with a blood disorder. Isabella saw how bravely he was putting up with his pain and she dropped everything to look after him. In their last eighteen months together Isabella never complained of her own ailments. She grew to

When John Bishop was asked how such a small and frail woman as Isabella (who was under five foot tall) could manage such punishing journeys, he replied that it was because she had 'the appetite of a tiger and the digestion of an ostrich'.

Isabella's husband, John Bishop. He was devoted to Isabella and was very understanding about her passion for travelling: 'I have only one formidable rival in Isabella's heart, and that is the high tableland of Central Asia.'

There was a time when I was altogether indifferent to missions, and would have avoided a mission-station rather than visited it. But the awful pressing claim of the un-Christianised nations, which I have seen, had taught me that the work of their conversion to Christ is one to which one would gladly give influence and whatever else God has given to one.

Isabella Bird Bishop (in a speech, 'Heathen Claims and Christian Duty', 1893)

love and worship John. She was devastated when, two days before their fifth wedding anniversary, he died.

On her own

Isabella wrote to her publisher that after the death of the two people whom she cared for most, she would never be as strong or have the same 'spirit' again. She decided to make one last journey. John had been a strong supporter of medical missionaries (they believed that the best way to bring the Christian God to non-believers was by giving medical help). Isabella, too, had become convinced that they had a most important role to play in spreading the Christian faith.

She decided to build a memorial to John in Asia in the form of a hospital. She would also make a tour of the missions, taking notes as she went. She did a short course in nursing and, early in 1889, set sail for Kashmir in northern India. From now on, Isabella would always set herself a practical goal, such as funding a hospital or an orphanage, for each new journey (she made several after this 'last' one). It was as if she now felt it was wrong to travel, as she had done in the past, just for the enjoyment and fascination of it.

She gradually became less tolerant of other people's lifestyles too. This was not just because she was growing older (she was now fifty-eight). Since the deaths of Hennie and John she had begun to rely more and more on the Christian religion for comfort and to give her life a sense of purpose. Other beliefs now seemed more of a threat and she was quicker to dismiss them as 'worthless'. Yet the people and landscapes of remote countries continued to fascinate her, and some of her toughest trips were to come.

Chapter Seven

Among the Tibetans

It was June by the time Isabella had organised the building of the John Bishop Memorial Hospital in Srinagar in Kashmir. The town was 'in season', the time when the British people who were working in the plains moved up into the cooler hills to avoid the worst of the summer heat. Isabella couldn't stand all the arrogant polo and tennis players there. So, with an Afghan soldier for a guide, she headed east towards the Himalayas and Ladakh. Ladakh was a part of western Tibet and one of the most remote regions Westerners were allowed to visit. The rest of Tibet was Chinese and kept its frontiers closed to all outsiders.

During the day the temperature rose to 55°c (130°F) and at night dropped below freezing point as they climbed the mountain ridges leading to Leh, the capital of Ladakh. 'I did not suffer from the climate,' Isabella remarks casually, 'but in the case of most Europeans the air passages become irritated, the skin cracks, and after a time the action of the heart is affected. The hair when released stands out from the head, leather shrivels and splits . . . food dries up.' Water colour sketching was 'nearly impossible' because the water evaporated so quickly.

Leh was a bustling trade centre where merchants from other parts of Kashmir, Afghanistan and Chinese Tibet gathered to sell their goods. Animals squealed and bellowed, traders shouted out their bargains at the top of their voices and wandering

The town of Leh, capital of Ladakh, 'huddled below a range of 18000-foot-high mountains and encircled by a plain of blazing-hot gravel'.

. . . my umbrella split to pieces, shoes and other things cracked, screws fell out of my camera . . . , my air cushion collapsed, a horn cup went to pieces spontaneously, and celluloid films became electric and emitted sparks when they were separated!

Isabella Bird Bishop (on the effects of high altitude)

musicians entertained the onlookers.

A German missionary called Mr Redslob, who had been living in the area for twenty-five years, was just setting off on a three-week tour of the northern province of Nubra. Isabella was delighted when he asked her to join him.

A Tibetan monk, four servants and two baggage-horse drivers made up the party. By nightfall they had climbed to a height of nearly 4900 metres. Blood trickled from the horses' nostrils as they gasped for breath. In the morning they were replaced by sturdy yaks which could cope with the thin mountain air. Isabella discovered that yaks were surprisingly nimble on the craggy slopes but had a nasty habit of kicking or dumping their riders whenever the mood took them.

Nubra was hotter and more fertile than

Ladakh, and the people simpler and more religious. Because of Mr Redslob's reputation for kindness and his skill with medicines, they were given a warm welcome everywhere.

Crossing the Shyok

They wandered around the mountain villages, heading south. In the valley of the Shyok river they remounted their horses. The river, which they had to cross, was rising rapidly as the glaciers further upstream melted in the summer heat. The Tibetans said prayers and made offerings for a cloudy day. But the sun blistered down and the Shyok rose higher and higher.

They plunged in. For half an hour the horses simply trod water, unable to push against the force of the river. Everyone shouted encouragement at the horses and finally Mr Redslob's mount surged forwards and up on to the bank. Isabella's horse was urged on, missed the bank and rolled over backwards into the river, trapping her under it. 'A struggle, a moment of suffocation and I was extricated by strong arms, to be knocked down again by the rush of water, to be again dragged up . . . the crumbling bank. I escaped with a broken rib and some severe bruises but the horse was drowned.'

Isabella took just one day's rest, in an apricot orchard (she never liked to hold up her fellow travellers). A few days later they reached the Buddhist monastery of Deskyid. Built on a mountain ridge, some 3300 metres up, it was an inspiring sight. Its red, white and yellow temples were dotted with flags, ornamental spears and yaks' tails. The hills echoed with a 'tornado of sound' produced by monster gongs, silver horns, cymbals and

It must be understood that all Tibetan literature is 'sacred', though some of the volumes of exquisite calligraphy on parchment . . . contain nothing better than fairy tales and stories of doubtful morality . . .

Isabella Bird Bishop

drums. Having climbed the zigzag stone steps to the front gate, Isabella remarked that it was 'well worth the crossing of the Shayok fords, my painful accident, and much besides'.

Strange customs
She warmed to the people of Nubra. She learnt about their ritual way of harvesting the grain (which involved chanting, making sacred symbols and offering a portion of grain to the axe). She also discovered what she called 'some curious features' of their family life. The most 'curious' of these was their practice of polyandry. This meant that only the eldest son of a family was allowed to marry, but his wife was expected to take all his brothers as inferior husbands. All her children, whether fathered by the eldest son or one of his brothers, were treated as the legal property of the eldest son.

Isabella noted down that this custom was the biggest obstacle to converting Tibetans to Christianity. However, her almost matter-of-fact reaction to this lifestyle showed that she could still be surprisingly open-minded. Most Victorian ladies, strictly brought up on the Christian idea of marriage, would have been shocked at the notion of a woman having several husbands. But Isabella found the Nubrans happy and friendly and perhaps she felt that their practice of polyandry was an important factor in their happiness. She even relates that the women thought a European woman's married life was terribly dull!

A golden opportunity
Not wanting to be trapped in Kashmir for the winter, Isabella headed south through the Punjab to the hill town of Simla. Here she

Isabella visited several monastic settlements, such as these, in the Himalayas. Some were built right on the peak of mountains and could only be reached by climbing hundreds of steps.

met Major Herbert Sawyer who was preparing for a geographical and military survey of western Persia (now Iran). Isabella had always wanted to visit Persia but had been warned against it — people said it was too dangerous, physically and politically. Both Britain and Russia were trying to exert their power there.

Isabella realised that Sawyer's offer to escort her to Tehran was an opportunity not to be missed. She knew that their partnership would not be ideal: Sawyer, who was a dashing thirty-eight year old, was quick tempered and something of a bully. She was a single-minded widow, twenty years older, who was used to making her own travel plans. This time she would certainly have preferred to travel alone. But she would put up with Sawyer in order to see Persia.

By January 1890 they had reached Baghdad in Iraq and were making their last-minute preparations for the 800-kilometre ride to Tehran. Sawyer strode through the bazaars, 'holding a handkerchief to his nose and looking utterly . . . disgusted at everything'. Isabella was nervous about riding a mule on an untried saddle, especially since she had developed rheumatism in her knees. Normally she was decisive and positive. This time, she wondered if she was making a bad mistake.

Chapter Eight

The Perils of Persia

The trek through Iraq to the Persian border was across bare plains. Icy winds swept down from snow-covered mountains. They were held up in a small town for a few days by the appalling weather. This gave Isabella a chance to take a close look at the daily life of a peasant couple with three children. Her descriptions of their wet and miserable existence are so vivid that you can almost feel the dampness creeping into your bones. The fire of twigs and thistles is so pathetic that the wife can only warm the porridge in the morning, not even bring it to the boil. She spends her whole day padding around the house in wet clothes doing chores. She must serve her husband the food first, followed by her son. Only then can she and her daughters eat the leftovers — at a respectful distance from the men.

Although this journey to Tehran was physically the toughest Isabella had experienced, what she found hardest to take was the appalling poverty and misery of the peasants. Under the Shah's corrupt system of government the poorer people were much more likely to be fined, humiliated or tortured than those who could afford to bribe their way out of punishment. Isabella was equally appalled at the brutality of the punishments — for example, anyone who stole a telegraph post (wood was very scarce) would be hung by one ear from a post in the middle of the desert.

Isabella herself was hardly living in the lap

The six woollen layers of my mask, my three pairs of gloves, my sheepskin coat, fur cloak, and mackintosh piled on over a swaddling mass of woollen clothing, were as nothing before that awful blast. It was not a question of comfort or discomfort, or of suffering more or less severe, but of life or death, as the corpses a few miles ahead of us show.

Isabella Bird Bishop (describing the trek from Baghdad to Tehran)

On her way from Tehran to Isfahan Isabella met a number of dervishes – Muslim holymen who walked the roads, telling fortunes, praying and begging. Some were quite frightening and Isabella nervously gave one shelter overnight.

of luxury. Her first night in Persia was typical of what she was to find all along the route. They stopped at a stable which was already packed with some four hundred mules and their drivers. The floor was ankle-deep with manure but Isabella was prepared to make do. As she started to find herself a corner in a manger, she was offered the only room in the village. It did have a door and a hole for a window but not much else. The floor was full of puddles, the roof leaked and she had to sleep with a waterproof sheet over her. Morning tea was made with 'slimy greenish water' from a ditch outside her room.

The road to Tehran was a bumpy track, only wide enough for one mule. At times they met other travellers and when neither party would give way a chaotic and dangerous struggle would follow. They rode about twenty-two kilometres a day in the searing cold. Once Isabella's hands were so numb that she had to be lifted off her saddle.

Nights were just as bad. The walls of the inn rooms were sometimes covered in icicles. Whenever they stopped, peasants would swarm around Isabella, pleading for cures for everything from eye cataracts, smallpox and tumours to epilepsy.

Life in the cities

Forty-six days after they had left Baghdad, Isabella and Sawyer stumbled into the British Legation in Tehran. Caked with mud, hardly able to walk, Isabella heard a formal English voice announcing, 'Dinner is waiting'. To her horror, she realised that a dinner party had been arranged in her honour. Mumbling apologies, she went straight to her room, threw off her cloak, collapsed in front of the fire and fell into a deep sleep.

She spent three weeks in Tehran. She was disappointed to find that the bazaars were stuffed with foreign goods. The women, it seemed to her, were 'shrouded formless bundles' creeping down alleys whereas the men strutted around, shouting, laughing, cheating. Isabella arranged to meet up with Sawyer in the city of Isfahan and headed south with an interpreter and cook.

Isfahan was not welcoming. On her way across the city Isabella was mocked and spat on by groups of men. The Isfahanis did not tolerate followers of any religion apart from Islam. Muslim women were not allowed to walk in the streets unchaperoned or unveiled, so nor could Isabella. She only managed one visit to the non-European part of the city and that was to the women in a harem.

From her descriptions, the lives of these women could not have been more different from Isabella's. Their rooms were lavishly decorated and they themselves were heavily made up. Most of them were overweight from eating too many sweets, and pale from no exercise or fresh air. They had nothing to do all day except gossip, concoct love potions and squabble. Isabella couldn't wait to get back to the mission where she was staying.

When she returned to London she spoke out passionately against what seemed to her the 'degradation' of women under Islam. Muslim women, she said, were not considered worth educating; their main function was to serve the man of the house whenever and however he wanted. Worst of all, she continued, was the fate of the women in the harems where 'all the worst passions of human nature are stimulated and developed in a dreadful degree: jealousy, envy, murderous hate, intrigue . . .'.

Whether 'formless bundles' or pampered and painted ladies of the harem, Isabella found the lot of women in Persia a miserable one.

Bakhtiari country

... the Sahib [Sawyer] ought to be most friendly and polite to the great feudal chief whose guest he is, and yet is most desperately insolent ... when the two sons of the Ilkhani called ... he coolly went out at once, saying to me, 'Now do the best you can with them!' After which he stood outside the tent within earshot ... making a snort of ridicule and saying sarcastic things in a whisper about my feeble efforts, which Mirza heard and kept giggling in his interpretation ... His behaviour is a frightful political mistake.

Isabella Bird Bishop

The Sahib [Sawyer] has just told me that I am to help him with the observations ... It is terribly hard work, my hands get shaky and icy cold and I get some very sharp words. A single mistake of sight and ... all the elaborate astronomical calculations will be upset.

Isabella Bird Bishop

At the end of April Isabella met up with Sawyer again. Although they were both strong-willed and, at times, stubborn, they had become 'good comrades'. Sawyer's mission was to survey the lands of the nomadic Bakhtiari to the south and west of Isfahan. A few days later they were in the wilds once more, wandering through the remote plains of Khuzistan. The Bakhtiari were more or less independent, and were rumoured to be cruel and treacherous.

Isabella was not enthusiastic about the Bakhtiari's nomadic way of life: 'its total lack of privacy, its rough brutality, its dirt, its undisguised greed ... are all painful on a close inspection.' But when they crowded around her tent, pleading for medicines, she felt it her Christian duty to help. Some days she saw up to two hundred patients, which must have been quite an ordeal. Sawyer used her too, as a mediator between himself and the tribal chiefs — she was more tactful and polite than the 'insolent' Sawyer. Then, when one of his surveyors fell ill, she had to help him with his geographical observations.

As they clambered up the mountain ranges the tribesmen they met were wilder and more dangerous. Twice, their party was fired on. Isabella was glad to get out of Bakhtiari country safely. She was also glad to say goodbye to Sawyer and his bad temper.

She travelled north to the city of Hamadan where she collapsed with a fever. From there she could have gone to Baghdad and caught a boat to Cairo. But, typically, she chose the overland route, a 1600-kilometre trek through north-west Persia and Turkey to Trebizond (now Trabzon) on the Black Sea.

At first she greatly enjoyed the company of

46

the Kurds she met — wild looking men and unveiled, attractive women. But later, in the mountains of Kurdistan, she met Syrian and Armenian Christian peasants and was shocked to be told that their communities had been robbed and terrorised by the Kurds. The Kurds were fiercely protective of the territory they claimed as theirs.

By the time Isabella reached Trebizond she had been in Persia for a year and was ready to head back to Edinburgh. She arrived in Scotland just after Christmas, thinking she would now settle down.

A photograph of Isabella (right) with two English missionaries outside her tent in Bakhtiari country.

47

Chapter Nine

Korea in Turmoil

Isabella's idea of settling down was to throw herself into a whirl of activities that would help the cause of medical missionaries. She gave public lectures all round the country and campaigned for the persecuted Armenian and Syrian Christians.

She spent two winters on Mull, organising cookery classes for the locals and giving 'improving' talks on subjects such as 'How to make home happy'. Away from the critical stare of society ladies, she felt able to throw on her warm serge petticoats, comfortable jerseys and man's heavy overcoat when she visited the islanders with her well-used medicine box.

She also lectured to geographers and politicians on the mainland about her Persian experiences. The Fellows of the Royal Geographical Society (RGS) were so impressed with her achievements that they elected her first woman Fellow of the society. It was a great honour.

Most people, though, still looked on women as inferior to men in intelligence, physical stamina and courage. At an RGS meeting in 1893 the question of allowing women members into the society was debated hotly. Some men sneered, saying that by allowing them in, the society had become little more than a garden party society. George Curzon, whom Isabella had met on the boat to Baghdad and who was later to become viceroy of India, was all in favour of expelling women, saying, 'Their sex

Mrs Bishop impressed me as being a woman of unusual gifts, not only as a speaker and writer, but also as an observer and collector of information, possessing so much courage and force of character as to make her practically fearless, undismayed by obstacles, and undeterred by physical weakness; and yet there was nothing of that masculinity which is a common feature of women who have made their mark in distinctively masculine fields of activity.

Rev W.G. Walshe (a missionary in China)

and training render them equally unfitted for exploration'.

Isabella, who had clearly disproved this view many times over, did not make any comment in public. But she did write to a friend that the proposals were a 'dastardly injustice to women'. In the end a vote was passed to allow those women Fellows who had already been elected with Isabella, to remain — but no other women were to be elected in future.

Since her experiences in Persia and Kurdistan Isabella had described the East as 'corrupt and vicious'. But she was still drawn to it. She must make another journey, she told herself, to report on the work of the missions in Korea and China. That was her official reason. But it is clear from the letters she wrote to friends that no matter how hard

she tried to lead a 'good' quiet life, as Hennie and John had done, she was not happy. What she longed for was to be on a horse once more, soaking up new sights, sounds and smells.

Although she was now what she called 'an old woman and stout', and had chest problems and rheumatism, she took a course in photography, packed two cameras with her other essentials, and set sail for Korea.

An ancient civilisation

Her first impressions were not good. The seedy port of Chemulpo, ringed by bare hills, was muddy and depressing. The people, she said, were 'indolent, cunning, limp and unmanly'. She journeyed to the capital Seoul. Again she saw filthy, crowded alleys and slums. But here she also saw splendid palaces; she watched straw-hatted peasants driving bulls loaded with pine brushwood and she smelt its aromatic smoke at night-time. She heard the songs of the coolies who carried the rickshaws and the deep clang of the city's bronze bells. Isabella was yet again recording an ancient civilisation that had only recently opened its ports to Western traders and she found it fascinating.

Buddhism had been Korea's official religion

Isabella spent five weeks on a 28-foot sampan in Korea. She made herself a dark room on board so that she could develop her negatives.

up until the sixteenth century but had then been rejected. However, there were still hundreds of monks, living in peaceful seclusion, in the Diamond Mountains north of Seoul. Accompanied by a missionary-interpreter called Mr Miller, Isabella set off to visit them.

She hired a sampan that had to be weighed down with thousands of low-value coins, known as *cash*, as well as tea, flour and charcoal. They floated along the River Han, meeting the friendly inhabitants of the mud-walled houses. Here Isabella was amazed to see mothers stuffing bowls of rice into young children. When they couldn't fit in any more sitting up, the mothers would lie the children down and cram in extra spoonfuls. To have a huge appetite, and to be rolling in fat, seemed to be the Korean peasant's ultimate ambition.

When Isabella took to the roads she discovered just how awful Korean inns could be — as hot as ovens, crawling with vermin and piled high with rotting beans and dirty clothes. But once she got into the mountains she was revitalised by the sheer beauty of the region. The monasteries had been built on lush plateaux. They were encircled by hills covered with a tangle of magnificent trees and brilliant shrubs. Majestic peaks of pink granite rose high above them. To Isabella the monks' religious performances were 'absolutely without meaning', but she was won over by their appreciation of nature and their peaceful lifestyle.

Japanese invasion

She returned to Chemulpo to discover that a war was imminent. Japanese troops had landed, ostensibly to help the Korean king

She usually rode in a sedan chair on her expeditions and, though generally very much exhausted when the close of the day came, she appeared to be tireless so long as anything of interest remained to claim her attention. She was very easy to entertain, and my batchelor establishment had no difficulty in supplying her wants, so long as she was provided with indigestible things in the way of pastry.

Rev W.G. Walshe (a missionary in China)

51

fight a group of rebels. But their real purpose was to expel the Chinese, who had been in control of the country, and to impose Japanese rule instead. Isabella was more or less forced by the British vice-consul to leave for her own safety — she later complained to her publisher about the 'grandmotherliness of consuls'!

With a few coins in her pocket and only the clothes she was wearing, she arrived in Chefoo on the north-east coast of China. Undaunted, she requested fresh supplies from the British consul and set off on another adventure, this time up the River Liao. She was hit by appalling floods and her boat was turned into a rescue service for stranded families. But she survived and by January 1895 she could return to Seoul where she had an audience with the King and Queen.

She obviously impressed them greatly for they slipped her a top-secret letter for the Foreign Office in London. She described the Queen as a hard, highly intelligent woman who preferred alliance with the Chinese than with the Japanese. The King, she said, was

By the time Isabella made her last trip to the Far East a vital part of her luggage was her cumbersome photographic equipment. The muddiness of the water in the Yangtze made developing a problem and printing was also a 'great difficulty and I only overcame it by hanging the printing frames over the side [of the boat]. When all these rough arrangements were successful, each print was a joy and a triumph.'

nervous and ineffectual. Nine months later the Queen had been assassinated by the Japanese and the King imprisoned.

Isabella had now been in the East for over a year but she found it 'quite impossible to tear myself away'. She wanted to carry on recording the political and social changes of the area. Her original purpose for the trip — to describe the work of Korean and Chinese missionaries — in the end only covered a tiny fraction of her notes.

She returned to China once more, and stayed with a missionary called the Reverend Walshe. His description of her is a reminder of what an extraordinarily courageous, almost fearless, woman she was and how these qualities helped her to be such a good travel writer. 'Even in the face of the largest and noisiest crowds, Mrs Bishop proceeded with her photography and observations as calmly as if she were inspecting some of the Chinese exhibitions in the British Museum.' And yet, he goes on approvingly, she had none of that 'masculinity which is so common a feature of women who have made their mark in distinctively masculine fields of activity.' Isabella, no doubt, would have been delighted with this description.

A photograph by Isabella of a magnificent Chinese rock temple at Li-fan Ting.

She spent the last months of 1895 exploring the north-west coast of Korea. She got as far as the town of Tokchon where the peasants were so poor they could not even afford rice. As she sat 'amidst the dirt, squalor, rubbish . . . of the inn yard . . . I felt Korea to be hopeless, helpless, a mere shuttlecock of certain great powers.'

However, she was cheered by the thought that there was still China to be seen, that 'mysterious continent which has been my dream from childhood'.

Chapter Ten

China, Morocco and Packed Trunks

By the time Isabella reached Shanghai at the mouth of the River Yangtze it was a very Western, cosmopolitan city. It was a natural gateway to the vast continent of China and one of the most sophisticated trading ports in the East. The European and American residents did not impress Isabella. They seemed to care little for China or the Chinese and spent most of their time, she remarked, on 'sport and other amusements'. What did impress her was the great Yangtze, coursing along for over 5500 kilometres and not yet fully explored.

Isabella's sailing boat on the Yangtze. It had a crew of sixteen oarsmen and a ship's master who brought along his wife and baby too. 'I halted for Sunday in this lovely bay, an arrangement much approved by the trackers [oarsmen] who employed the holiday in washing their clothes, smoking a double quantity of opium, and making a distracting noise, aggravated by the ceaseless yell of boat baby.'

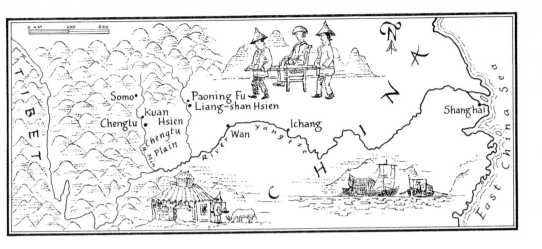

Isabella was the only foreigner to board a
modern river steamer (she would have much
preferred a traditional salt junk, she said)
bound for the city of Ichang, 1600 kilometres
upstream. Here goods were transferred from
steamers to junks and vice versa. Isabella
swapped her steamer for a proper sailing
boat.

It was good to be travelling at her own pace
again. As the landscape grew wilder and
more dramatic, Isabella observed and wrote
with the eyes of a cameraman and the ears of
a sound recordist. The river, she tells us, is
now chanelled between the nearly
perpendicular cliffs of the Ichang gorge.
Where the cliffs are a little less sheer, houses
have been built on minute platforms of rock.
Small children are tied to posts to prevent
them falling over the cliff edge. Above and
below the houses are pockets of cultivated
land 'not larger than a bath towel'; mauve
primulas and bright green ferns spring up
from sheltered crevices.

This 'region of mystery and magic' soon
changes to a place of danger where she spots
the wreckage of boats that have not made it

upstream. She is at the foot of a series of terrifying rapids and for once her nerves are not quite up to it. The jostling, noisy crowd of boatmen and trackers (hired to haul the boats up the rapids with ropes from the shore) annoy her as she waits, hour after hour, for her boat's turn to be taken up.

Certainly, the Chinese are more openly hostile to her, as they are to nearly all foreigners at the time, than any other peoples she has met. But she herself is also less tolerant and less flexible. This perhaps makes the situation worse. She describes them as 'repulsive', 'coarse' and 'brutal' and even wonders if they are 'made in the image of God'. It is interesting to compare this to her enthusiastic reaction, twenty years earlier, to the 'godless' Ainus.

Isabella's oarsmen at dinner: '. . . balancing their bowls on the tips of the fingers of the left hand close under the chin, the mouths are opened as wide as possible, and the food is shovelled in with the chopsticks as rapidly as though they were eating for a wager.'

'Foreign devil'

Her boat, with seventy men heaving and straining, was finally pulled up without disaster. She disembarked at Wan, aiming to reach the city of Paoning Fu, some 480 kilometres to the west. She was either becoming careless or dangerously arrogant for she did two very foolish things on this stretch of the journey. She rode in an open chair (most female missionaries knew that it was much wiser to use a covered one) and she wore a Japanese-style hat. Since the Chinese had recently been defeated by the Japanese in Manchuria, wearing a Japanese hat could easily be taken as an insult.

Three days out of Wan Isabella was attacked by a mob as she rode into the town of Liang-shan Hsien. The howling crowd yelled 'foreign devil' and 'child eater', threw mud and lashed out at her with their fists. She took refuge in a room which the crowd of some two thousand then tried to set alight. They had nearly broken down the door when soldiers arrived and ensured her safety for the rest of the night. It must have been a terrifying experience and Isabella does admit that she was strongly tempted to turn back. But, courageous as ever, and encouraged by the loyalty of her coolies, she forged ahead.

At the town of Paoning Fu she stayed at the China Inland Mission. There she arranged for a hospital to be set up in memory of Hennie. When she reached Kuan Hsien on the Chengtu plain there were no more missions for her to visit. But what about those tempting, snow-covered mountain peaks that led to the border with Tibet? Isabella couldn't resist them and set off, up into the lush hills. Determined as ever, she

The men asserted . . . that with my binoculars and camera I could see the treasures of the mountains, the gold, precious stones, and golden cocks which lie deep down in the earth; that I kept a black devil in the camera, and that I liberated him at night, and that he dug up the golden cocks, and that the reason why my boat was low in the water was that it was ballasted with these . . . fowls, and with the treasures of the hills!

Isabella Bird Bishop (in China)

Isabella took this photograph of a beggar woman who lived in a mat hut on the banks of the Han: 'These wretched beings have one solace in life – the opium pipe – and they starve themselves to procure it.' Isabella's crew smoked opium every night and although she did not approve of it she recognised their need for an escape from their grim lives: 'They might be better clothed and fed if they were not opium smokers, but then where would be their nightly Elysium?'

dealt firmly with two attempts by officials to stop her going into the mountains. She also survived a blizzard which hit them as they crossed a mountain pass 3600 metres up. Even at sixty-four, she thrived on that mixture of danger, discomfort and joy which travel involved. She pulled herself out of snowdrifts and stumbled down into a rich green valley, where she found the town of Somo. This was to be her most westerly port of call in China.

White haired but still dynamic

Back in England, after three years in the East, she rented rooms in London and rushed around, giving lectures on China and Korea and on the need for medical missions. She was still amazingly energetic. French and photography lessons were fitted in and she ordered a tricycle for exercise. After a few years, she started talking about another trip to China but her doctor strongly advised against it. She settled for Morocco instead. 'I am taking for rest,' she said, 'photography, embroidery and water-colours.'

Once she reached the Moroccan coast 'rest' didn't feature at all. The sea was so rough she had to be craned off the steamer into a small boat in a coal basket. At Marrakesh she was lent a black charger that was so big she had to mount him by ladder. She rode into the Atlas Mountains to meet the Berber sheiks. In a letter to a friend she said, 'You would fail to recognise your infirm friend astride on a

The public fountains in a Moroccan city, photographed by Isabella.

superb horse in full blue trousers and a short full skirt, with great brass spurs belonging to the generalissimo of the Moorish army.' She was chased by armed bandits and had a secret rendezvous with the young Sultan who told her, 'he hoped when his hair was as white as mine, he might have as much energy as I have!' Nearly seventy, Isabella still made a strong impression wherever she went.

She returned to England in the autumn of 1901, refuelled for further canvassing on behalf of medical missions. But by the summer of 1902 she knew that she had a serious heart disease. She went to Edinburgh and spent the last two years of her life moving from one nursing home to another. She died on 7 October 1904. Her packed trunks were in London, ready for that last journey to China she was hoping to make.

High priestess

Isabella Bird Bishop's natural vocation was that of born traveller in an age when the majority of women rarely moved beyond their family circle. The sights, sounds and customs of a new country, the challenge of a soaring mountain peak, the thrill of galloping alone across wild prairies — these were the things that gave meaning to her life.

From an early age she longed to be independent, to be free from the many restrictions that tied down most women of her time. Through single-minded determination, fighting crippling back pain for much of her life, Isabella won herself this freedom — able to roam, unchaperoned, to little known corners of the world. By doing this, she proved that a woman had the right 'to do what she can do well'.

A statue of Lin-Yang, Chinese god of thunder, taken by Isabella. On her travels Isabella encountered religious beliefs very different from her own. Initially fairly tolerant, as she grew older she became more typically Victorian in her dismissal of any faith other than Christianity.

Through her detached and detailed observations of remote peoples and their countries, she won the respect of Britain's top geographers and explorers. Her dramatic accounts of her exploits opened up exciting new worlds for thousands of ordinary people in Britain who read her books.

Her physical stamina, courage and energy were remarkable, even on her last trip at the age of sixty-nine. Neither extremes of cold or heat, man-eating tigers, floods, blizzards, violent mobs nor the threat of war could discourage her. It is no wonder that she was regarded as the high priestess of Victorian women travellers and that her life was an inspiration to all those who were to follow in her daring footsteps.

. . . she was a 'born traveller' — she told her tales well, she seldom retraced her steps, she never outstayed her welcome.

Pat Barr,
A Curious Life for a Lady,
1970

TIME CHART

1831 Isabella Bird born in Boroughbridge, N. Yorks. When she is small the family moves to Tattenhall, Cheshire. In 1835 they move again, to Birmingham.

1848 The Birds settle in Wyton, Huntingdonshire. Shortly afterwards Isabella has operation on spine.

1854 Isabella travels to Canada and North America

1856 Isabella's first book, *The Englishwoman in America*, published anonymously.

1858 Isabella's father dies. Two years later Isabella moves to Edinburgh. In 1866 her mother dies.

1869 Isabella very poorly. Doctors suggest sea trip. Voyage to New York and back does not help.

1872 Isabella sets off for Australia.

1873 Lands on Sandwich Islands. Climbs Mauna Loa. Then sails for San Francisco. Heads for the Rockies where she meets Jim Nugent.

1874 Returns to England.

1878 Arrives in Japan. Stays with Ainus. Returns via Hong Kong, China and Malay States.

1879 Arrives in Mull in May. A year later Hennie dies.

1881 Marries John Bishop.

1886 John Bishop dies.

1889 Sets off for Kashmir. Nearly drowns crossing Shyok river. From there travels south to Baghdad and then across Persia. Explores wild Bakhtiari country.

1890 Returns to London at Christmas.

1892 Elected first woman Fellow of Royal Geographical Society.

1894 Sets off for Korea and China. Gets caught up in Sino/Japanese war.

1896 Reaches Shanghai and ascends River Yangtze. Attacked by Chinese mob.

1897 Returns to England.

1900 *Chinese Pictures: Notes on photographs made in China* published by Cassell.

1901 Spends nine months in Morocco where she meets the Sultan.

1902 Moves to Edinburgh and stays in various nursing homes.

1904 Isabella dies on October 7, aged 72.

Isabella's Ainu host, Shinondi, and his friend. They used their bows and arrows to hunt bears which provided them with meat, skins and fat for lamps.

Acknowledgements

The author would like to thank the publishers John Murray Ltd for permission to quote from original letters and for assistance with illustrations.

The publishers would like to thank the following for supplying photographs and prints for use in this book:

The BBC Hulton Picture Library cover (above); The British Library pages 6, 8, (above and below), 10, 12, 13, 23, 36, 38, 41, 47, 58, 61; John Murray Limited pages 2, 14, 18, 19, 21, 31, 33, 44, 45, 50, 52, 53, 54, 56, 59, 63; *Punch* page 16.

Index

Further Reading

Current editions of books by Isabella Bird Bishop

A Lady's Life in the Rocky Mountains
(Virago Travellers, London 1982)
Unbeaten Tracks in Japan
(Virago Travellers, London 1982)
The Golden Chersonese and the Way Thither
(Century Travellers, London 1983)
The Yangtze Valley and Beyond
(Virago Travellers, London 1985)

Books about Isabella Bird Bishop

A Curious Life for a Lady, The Story of Isabella Bird, Traveller Extraordinary by Pat Barr
(Martin Secker and Warburg, London 1970;
Penguin Books, London 1985)
Victorian Lady Travellers by Dorothy Middleton
(Routledge and Kegan Paul, London 1965)
This Grand Beyond, The Travels of Isabella Bird Bishop selected by Cicely Palser Havely
(Century Publishing, London 1984)